D0204508

T 5996

This time Alfonse found a very good hiding place.

I see you!

The next day, Little Bird asked to play hide-and-seek again.

Only if you promise
to find me this time!
said Alfonse.

I promise.

I knew you would find me! *Little Bird said when she awoke.*

You were supposed to find <u>me</u>! *said Alfonse.*

Oh.

Akridge knack Free Public Library

Shhh! *whispered* Alfonse.
She's sleeping!

LOOK, EVERYONE,
I FOUND LITTLE BIRD!

Little Bird was tired of
playing. She sat down
by the lake to wait
and soon fell asleep.

So the geese looked in the water.

Here I am!
said Little Bird.
But <u>still</u> no one heard her.

Maybe Little Bird
went in the water.

HONK!

Where are you, Little Bird?

The geese helped Alfonse look.

HONK!

HONK!

HONK!

HONK!

HONK!

Here I am!

said Little Bird.
But no one heard her.

HELP! HELP! *he cried to the other geese.*
I've lost Little Bird!

Alfonse began to look for Little Bird.

LITTLE BIRD!
LITTLE BIRD!

OH, NO! *said Alfonse.*
WHERE COULD LITTLE BIRD BE?

LITTLE BIRD,
WHERE ARE YOU?

**Hee,
hee,
hee!**

*giggled Little Bird, but
Alfonse didn't hear her.*

But Little Bird didn't return.

HERE I AM!

honked Alfonse.

The hiding place was <u>so</u> good, and Alfonse was <u>so</u> quiet, that Little Bird walked right past him!

Alfonse waited and waited.

Come out, come out, wherever you are!

Birdsville Free Public Library

Then he found a place,
and just in time.
Little Bird was coming!

So Alfonse kept looking.

no rock was big enough,

and no grass was tall enough.

Alfonse was looking for a good hiding place, but...

no
tree
was
wide
enough,

ARE YOU?

ALFONSE, WHERE

Ready or not, here I come!

For David and Alan

Copyright © 1996 by Linda Berkowitz Wikler
All rights reserved. No part of this book may be reproduced or
transmitted in any form or by any means, electronic or mechanical,
including photocopying, recording, or by any information storage and
retrieval system, without permission in writing from the publisher.

Published by Crown Publishers, Inc., a Random House company,
201 East 50th Street, New York, NY 10022

CROWN is a trademark of Crown Publishers, Inc.

Manufactured in Singapore

Library of Congress Cataloging-in-Publication Data
Wikler, Linda.
Alfonse, where are you? / by Linda Wikler. — 1st ed.
        p.   cm.
Summary: Alfonse the goose can't find Little Bird when they play
hide-and-seek, but if he were quiet, he might be able to hear her.
[1. Hide-and-seek—Fiction. 2. Geese—Fiction. 3. Birds—Fiction.]
I. Title.
PZ7.W6415Al   1996
[E]—dc20 95-3670

ISBN   0-517-70045-X (trade)
         0-517-70046-8 (lib. bdg.)

10 9 8 7 6 5 4 3 2 1

First Edition

ALFONSE, WHERE ARE YOU?

Linda Wikler

Crown Publishers, Inc., New York

You won't find me!

1, 2, 3, 4...

DATE DUE		
SEP 19 1996		
5/11/00		
10/31/02		

preschool

DISCARD

Norridgewock Free Public Libr...

Norridgewock Public Library

Norridgewock, Maine

1. Books may be kept two weeks and may be renewed once for the same period, except 7 day books and magazines.

2. A fine is charged for each day a book is not returned according to the above rule. No book will be issued to any person incurring such a fine until it has been paid.

3. All injuries to books beyond reasonable wear and all losses shall be made good to the satisfaction of the Librarian.

4. Each borrower is held responsible for all books charged on his card and for all fines accruing on the same.